Little Leila
and
the big table

Written by PJ McIlvaine
Illustrated by Leila Nabih

Little Lena and The Big Table

Copyright 2019 © Text-Pj McIlvaine, Art-Leila Nabih

Published by
Big Belly Book Co.
Richmond, Texas 77406
www.bigbellybookco.com

ISBN - 978-1-7325541-4-6
LCN - 2019906289
Printed and Bound in the United States of America.

www.bigbellybookco.com

To my big brother Mikey, who sat with me at the little kid's table.
He complained that I always got the bigger slice of pizza, never shared, and burped on command.

-Pj (Your Pat Pat)

Lena loved when the entire family got to visit. Birthdays, holidays, Easter...

Every Thanksgiving, there would be a huge feast: roast turkey, gravy, mashed potatoes, and Uncle Ron's famous pumpkin pie.

Lena didn't like however:

Aunt Toni's fried pickle casserole...

... and Gampy's corny jokes.

But most of all, Lena hated sitting at the little kid's table.

Andy created his own marshmallow challenge.

Margaret juggled dessert like a circus trapeze artist.

Penelope tried to be a one-armpit band.

Each year, no matter how hard Lena pleaded to sit at the big table with the grown-ups, the answer was always the same.

"You're too little, Lena. Next year," Ganny would say.

But Ganny...

Mom would shoo Lena over to the little kid's table.

But Mom....

But that was last year. "This year will be different,"
Lena insisted. Lena was determined to show
everyone just how big she was.

They'd HAVE TO let her sit at the big table.

"What a big helper you are," Mom said.

"You're such a big girl," Ganny said.

"Boy, you're so big and strong," Dad said with a chuckle.

Lena tugged on Ganny's apron.

Now can I sit at the big table?

Maybe next year, sweetie.

Lena sulked. Not again!

Suddenly, an ear splitting screech filled the room.

Waaaaaaaa.....!

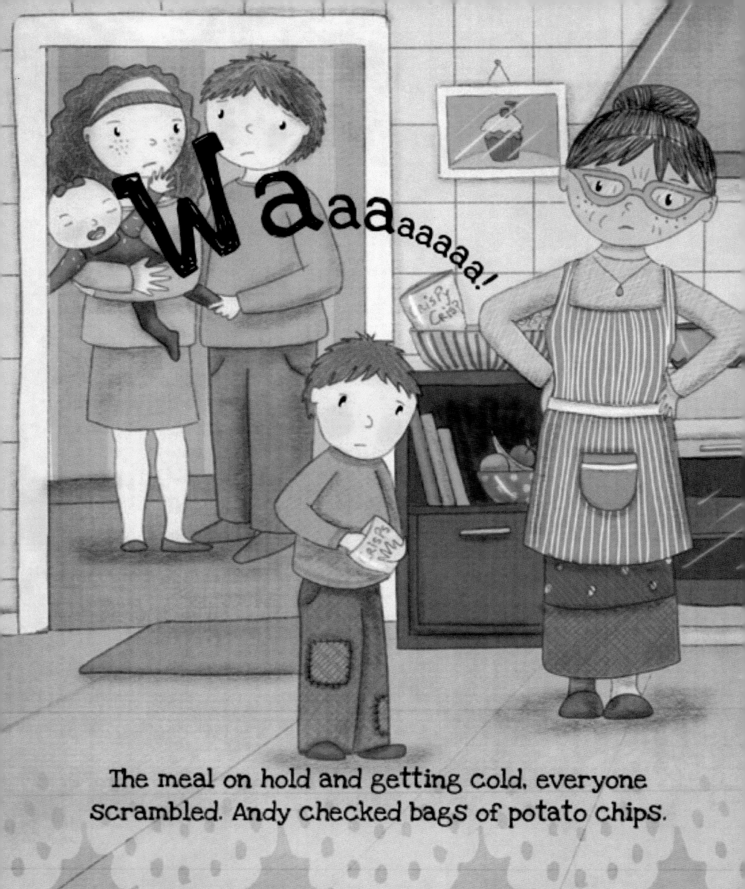

The meal on hold and getting cold, everyone scrambled. Andy checked bags of potato chips.

Suddenly, Lena had a **brilliant** idea...

Baby Sandra cooed over Lena's lovey.
Everyone ahhhed.

Lena felt very grown up sitting at the big table.
This was the place to be!

But she soon realized.....

Ganny took out her teeth and complained about her sore gums.

Mom shared embarrassing photos....

This is soooo boring...

Uncle Ron spit when he spoke.

Lena frowned.... ugghhh....

Lena glanced over at the
little kid's table.

Andy gushed like
a fountain.

Penelope played
Lena's favourite

Lena was missing **all** the fun.

That **WAS** the place to be !!!

"Maybe next year."

57442559R00020

Made in the USA
Middletown, DE
30 July 2019